A Pocketful of Kisses

by Angela McAllister
illustrated by Sue Hellard

BLOOMSBURY
CHILDREN'S
BOOKS

A Pocketful of Kisses

For Ginny – A.M.

With special thanks to the Reception Class of 2003/04
at Oakthorpe School, Enfield – S.H.

BLOOMSBURY
CHILDREN'S
BOOKS

First published in Great Britain in 2006 by Bloomsbury Publishing Plc
36 Soho Square, London, W1D 3QY

This paperback edition first published in 2007

Text copyright © Angela McAllister 2006
Illustrations copyright © Sue Hellard 2006
The moral rights of the author and illustrator have been asserted

A CIP catalogue record of this book is available from the British Library

ISBN 978 0 7475 7304 3

Printed in China by South China Printing Co

1 3 5 7 9 10 8 6 4 2

All papers used by Bloomsbury Publishing are natural, recyclable products
made from wood grown in well-managed forests. The manufacturing processes
conform to the environmental regulations of the country of origin.

The first day Digby went to school he learnt how to line
up in the playground, where to hang his jacket and how
to say, "Yes, Mrs Hoot," when the teacher called his name.
He played with sand, sang rhymes and painted a picture
for Mum.

"Did you have a good time?" asked Dad.
"Yes," said Digby.

Next morning, Mum opened the curtains.

"Time to get up for school."

"No," said Digby. "I went there yesterday."

"You have to go again," explained Mum gently. "You're a schoolboy now."

"No, I'm not. I'm a homeboy," said Digby. "I want to stay here with you."

And he hid under the bedclothes.

But Digby did have to go.

"Why are you worried?" asked Mum as they walked to school through the wood.

"I've forgotten where to line up and where to hang my jacket," said Digby. "I might not hear the teacher when she calls my name."

"I'll be there to put you in line," said Mum.

Digby wrinkled his nose unhappily. "I want you to stay all day."

"No," said Mum. "I can't do that."

When they got to school Digby stopped at the gate.

"I'm not going without you."

Mum gave him a hug. Then she had an idea. She cupped her hands, blew a dozen kisses and slipped them into Digby's pocket.

"There! If you're worried, take a kiss from your pocket and imagine I am with you."

Digby squeezed her tight.

"Ooops ... don't squash them!" said Mum.

The school bell rang and all the children lined up and went inside. Digby kept his jacket on.

When Mrs Hoot called his name, he answered loud and clear.

But when it was time to choose partners for a clapping game, Digby felt shy.

He dipped a finger into his pocket and pressed it to his cheek. It felt warm, just like a kiss from Mum. Digby smiled.

"Will you be my partner?" asked a little girl called Otterly.

"Yes," said Digby, and they clapped together.

At playtime, Digby sat on the bench. All the other children ran about happily. But nobody asked him to join in.

Once more Digby took a kiss from his pocket.
He imagined Mum beside him and felt
a little bit braver.
Digby stood up
and took a
step forward.

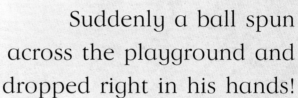

Suddenly a ball spun
across the playground and
dropped right in his hands!

"Throw it back!" called
the other children.
"Come and play!"

After play, Mrs Hoot read a story and the class talked about it. Digby even put up his hand to answer a question.

We all eat

different food.

Have you found your bag?

walk, don't run!

But, at lunchtime, there were lots of things to remember.

"Boys and girls with lunch boxes on that table. Children having school lunch, line up here. Fetch your drinks from the tray on the trolley. Don't start eating until everyone is sitting down," said Mrs Hoot.

Digby felt worried again. A teardrop prickled his eye.
If only Mum was there to tell him what to do. Once
more he took a kiss from his pocket and pressed it
to his cheek. Then he rubbed that teardrop away.

"Digby," said Mrs Hoot, "you come and sit here beside me."
And she showed him just what to do.

After lunch was playtime again. Everyone took off their jackets in the warm sun. One of the boys gave Digby the ball, so he took off his jacket too.

He was soon having great fun.

In the afternoon, Mrs Hoot asked the children one at a
time to stand up and tell the class about their family.
Digby didn't want to stand up in front of everyone.
He slipped away to get his jacket.

Digby found his jacket in the playground. But when he put it on he saw the pocket was ripped! He put his finger through the hole. The pocket felt cold and empty.

"The kisses have fallen out!" gasped Digby. His little nose began to quiver. Just then he heard someone sobbing. It was Otterly.

"What's the matter?" asked Digby, blinking away a tear of his own.

"I can't find the water fountain," said Otterly, "and I'm too shy to ask."

"I know where it is," said Digby. "I saw it at lunchtime."

Digby took Otterly to the water fountain, then they went back to class together.

"Can I sit next to you, Digby?" whispered Otterly.

"Yes," said Digby and he pulled a chair up close.

For the rest of the day
Otterly sat beside Digby
and he looked after her.
He sharpened her pencil,

found her an apron,

and explained things
she didn't understand.

Digby completely forgot about the pocketful of kisses
until it was time to go home.

Mum was waiting at the gate. She gave Digby a hug.

"Can I come back tomorrow?" he said. "I've got a
new friend."

"Did you need your pocket of kisses?" asked Mum.
Digby showed her the pocket.

"They fell out," he said with a frown.

Just then Otterly appeared wearing exactly the same jacket as Digby!

"You've got mine," she said, laughing. "I caught the pocket on my bicycle coming to school."

Digby and Otterly swapped.

"See you tomorrow," they said.

After tea Digby hung his satchel on the end
of his bed.

"I don't think I'll need a jacket tomorrow,"
he decided with a yawn.

"Oh, good," said Mum, tucking him in. "But
I hope schoolboys aren't too grown up for a
goodnight kiss?"

"Not me," said Digby happily. "Never!"